The
Kissing Room

To My Father
To My Devoted Husband
&
To Byron,
Whose poem *When We Two Parted* inspired this story.

In secret we met,
In silence I grieve,
That thy heart could forget,
Thy spirit deceive.
If I should meet thee
After long years,
How should I greet thee?
With silence and tears.

CHERYL ANNE GARDNER

The
Kissing Room

A Twisted Knickers Publication

1

A Shot *in the Dark*

I t looked like any one of a thousand unremarkable
nights. The lingering smell of lager and smoke. The
murky haze. The glistening glassware, and the bar
lights casting a dim glow from the fake Tiffany shades.
Nothing at all seemed out of the ordinary, except the
silence, menacing and oppressive, drip, drip, dripping
from the walls in the damp come from the bricks.

Long shadows aside, there was this ache I felt. It had
started in my chest earlier in the evening and had grown
into a twisted dread, drilling into the pit of my stomach
as I neared the men's toilets. I wasn't prepared, but
nothing really could have prepared me for the millions
of justifications and denials that my mind would put
forward in order to erase that moment to come from all
time in perpetuity: past, present, and future.

They always say that the world seems to move in slow motion and that your life passes in front of your eyes when confronted with what can only be defined as The End. That is what they say, and I can officially say it's absolute rubbish.

Who in the hell are *they* anyway?

They are outsiders.

Day-trippers.

Tourists, offering cheap compassion and a multitude of clichés to dull their own sense of mortality. For all their thoughts and prayers, they can't feel what you feel, can't know what you know or understand what you are going through. They can't even begin to interpret the vile and unspeakable thoughts come to slither about in your head. That sort of pain is yours alone.

You own it, and it owns you.

As I stood there staring at the blood-covered walls, nothing flashed before my eyes. Nothing came into my mind. The fact that I could no longer breathe was the only thing even remotely perceptible to me. There were no words, no tears, and no heartfelt moans. I just stared at it. A cold, dark, and empty stare. The same stare I had at my husband Jonathan's funeral a week later. The same stare that became a permanent part of me from that moment forward. My entire world had gone to wrack and ruin in Jon's one brief moment of clarity.

You can never really know what's going through a person's mind at the exact moment they decide to end their existence. That's their pain, and if they survive the endeavour, they'll never tell you. If they succeed, all you can do is pick up the pieces and attempt to go on, but every night, as I lay reaching towards the empty space in our bed, I just couldn't fathom how to do that, how to pick up the shattered pieces of my life and get on with it.

I felt ashamed, somehow responsible, and the guilt I felt was beyond measure. The void he left behind filled the gaping holes in my heart with the same cold, empty, silence I'd experienced that night.

One day went by, then another, and then the days, months, and years after that became a blurry incoherent collage of disconnected moments. I spent a great deal of time staring into the bottom of a whiskey bottle. I didn't sleep much, and I recall some time spent in a psychiatric hospital, some ridiculousness relating to shock and other medical gibberish about my mental state. A danger to myself, they said.

Maybe, probably. Who knows?

In my opinion—and I have lots of those—there was nothing wrong with my mental state. The facts were the facts: Jonathan was dead; I was guilty of a mountain of indiscretions; I was convinced that my redemption was at hand; and, I was going to take whatever punishment the universe saw fit to deal me.

Psychotherapy wasn't going to change the situation or release me from the festering hatred that had come, without resistance, to consume me alive. Drugs, which I adamantly refused, just dull the pain, and that clearly defeats the purpose of it all. Forgetting someone you never thought you'd lose is pain that must be endured, so I was not suicidal. The notion never entered into my mind. I didn't want to die. If I were supposed to die, I figured it would happen when it was right, in the grand scheme of things.

I simply didn't want to be alive.

Kafka once wrote, 'A first sign of the beginning of understanding is the wish to die.' For the first time in my life, I understood what he meant.

2

Last Call *and the Drifter*

I moved to Ireland in my early thirties in order to help my father run the family pub, just as he had done years before for his father. It wasn't really a choice but more that I felt obligated in some way. On the other hand, it seemed a bit exciting and not such a dire career option when compared to a lot of other choices. Be your own boss, that sort of thing, not to mention that pub-crawling is the number one local pastime in Ireland, so the travel brochures say.

You see, a pub isn't just a place to have a drink and a bit of rustic food. They are not dank dirty dells of sorrow and desperation either, even if they make them seem that way in movies and books. Sluggards drowning their id and ego—their inadequacies and insecurities—in a glass of liquid cirrhosis. Pubs are much more than that.

They are Churches. Cathedrals. They are theatres for storytelling and song. Meeting places for lamenting lovers. Homes away from home for weary travellers, and their patrons are the keepers of the spirit of the village—the keepers of its history, the soul of its peoples, and its life's breath. Even in a small out-of-the-way village like ours, one could still make an adequate and respectable living as a pub-owner.

My father once said that he thought the occupation suited me, as I had an almost unnatural finesse for handling strangers. I didn't see it that way at all. I felt it was more of an adaptation than a genuine talent, a manipulation more than artistic finesse. I never felt I had much in the way of talent, and much like my father, I suffered my existence, and it never really bothered me in the least that I saw myself that way, until I met Jon.

Both my father and grandfather passed-on a long time ago, and so I worked the pub with the assistance of my father's long time friend, Henry.

For me, the pub was a wonderful distraction. So many people with stories. So many voices. Every night of the week was tantalizingly different. The din was so loud, it was deafening actually—utter and complete bedlam—and since Jon's death, it was the only place I could have peace from my own thoughts. I rarely left the confines of its walls.

I had met Jonathan in this very pub.

When you work in a liquor-serving establishment, you get used to the types of people who frequent them, and they are as mixt and mottled as the weather: cocky, contemptuous, sorrowful, depraved, criminal, and of course, the annoyingly happy-go-lucky people who make your life seem even more miserable and pathetic by comparison.

Jonathan didn't fit well into any of those categories though. Jonathan was unexpected and unlike anyone I had ever met perched over a glass in this place. He was, in my mind, true perfection, and his gentle and agreeable nature touched me so deeply that I felt like I'd fallen in love the moment our eyes met.

He had been in town that day on business, filing some local tax papers for the tailor down the street. He sat at the bar, neatly pressed and proper, and in a barely audible voice, he ordered a bit of lunch—chips, just a plate of chips—and a pint. Other than his order, he said nothing, rarely looked up from his plate, overpaid for his meal, and then left, leaving only a trace of his aftershave in the air. I never expected to see him again, but from that day forward, due to folly or fancy, he became a regular fixture in the afternoons and at weekends.

I remember how dreadfully uncomfortable he seemed in his own skin, fidgety, a touch sensitive to the abrasiveness of the world, allergic even, and he attempted, unsuccessfully so, to conceal that fact with a soft-spoken caginess. It gave him an awkward grace, which, instead of coming off clumsy or comical was delightful and charming.

He was lithesome and extraordinarily tall despite his slight build. His pale skin, like moonlight, set off the dark hair that fell over his forehead, and his painfully shy smile was a heartfelt smile that had to be earned, one that was quite remarkable at putting me off my guard and leaving me breathless.

But of all his features, his eyes were probably the most impressive. Soulful they were, focused yet soft, betraying every emotion he had. Even his ultra-studious wire-rimmed glasses could not detract from their beauty. He could look into the very depths of your being, and secretly, you wanted him to. He used to call his eyes 'puddles of mud' and had said often that he wished they were green. I couldn't have disagreed more.

You could talk to Jon for hours about nothing while staring into those eyes. His honest easiness drew people in, and his reverent manner told of a humble man who was genuinely captivated by whatever anyone had to say. His voice was deep and soft as a whisper, no matter what tone he had chosen to take. No, Jon wasn't pretentious. It wasn't his style. He was proper polite, a gentleman consistently in manner and appearance. No bellowing with laughter or screaming with anger. His emotions were always incredibly subtle in a preternatural way. Tranquil. Grounding. The very opposite of my own.

I am more of a rogue bohemian-gypsy, crass, but always honest. We were quite the pair.

Love settled over us in an instant, but Jon, an accountant by trade, had to have everything done up in a very orderly fashion, abiding by all appropriate and respectable timetables. Our whirlwind courtship was a reasonable year before we were married. Jon said that we were going to have the most fabulous life we could ever imagine, and given that being with him was enough for me, life was already pretty fabulous. Our wedding day on the cliffs was the happiest I had ever been in the whole of my life ... the wind catching the lace of my dress, the headiness of the lavender in my hair, the way Jon kept tugging at his bowtie ... and then we descended into darkness. The kind of darkness one never anticipates as they gaze into the eyes of their lover and say, "I do."

It's been five years since Jonathan killed himself and left me alone in this very *un*-fabulous existence. Colour vanished as life and all its infinite beauty gradually became nothing more than unremarkable, uninspiring shades of grey.

Anyway, my mind gets away from me more often now. Today. Yes, today: a rainy and cool evening. A spring evening at the ides of March was as typical an evening as one might expect, and the mood was not dramatically unlike many other evenings before it. The pub was full of raucous folks letting out a bit of steam. People were having polite conversations; long lost friends were catching up; and even some of the local criminals were having at a game of pool. Everyone seemed to be enjoying his or her own little slice of alcohol-induced reality, including myself.

Henry was at the end of the bar chatting exuberantly with a couple of patrons, waiving his pipe in the air as if he were narrating an eloquent memoir, and I was quietly observing the various scenarios playing out around me.

The pool game was getting fairly interesting. There was a little shoving, a little cussing, and a few loosely thrown accusations of cheating.

Maybe it would escalate.

I lived for breaking up bar fights. The risk of getting my head bashed in always made it a worthwhile bit of sport for me. Henry often said, "Stop being so aggressive and reckless. One of these days you'll wind up getting yourself killed." Henry lectured me often about my behaviour. Getting killed was a bit melodramatic I thought, but a girl could hope—couldn't she?

Reckless I was, but I wasn't a feckin eejit. Admittedly though, I have my moments. Lapses in discretion had become commonplace. Regardless, I always carried my hunting knife with me. Being relegated to cutting boxes and other bar sundries had tarnished it some, but it remained by my side ever vigilant nonetheless. Under the bar, we kept the shooters for those more difficult negotiations with drunken patrons. I seldom worried about whether or not I would be prepared for a bar fight, a political uprising, or a zombie apocalypse.

As I carefully assessed my position and effective reaction distance, I took a quick glance across the room, and in what seemed like a never-ending moment in time, I saw Jonathan seated at the end of the bar—he as much aware of me as I was of him.

This wasn't out of the ordinary either. I believed I had witnessed visions of Jonathan many times in the past, particularly right after his death, but this time was different. This was no figment of my imagination, no ruse, no trick of the light *or* the liquor. I'd had a few nips of whiskey here and there earlier in the evening, but I wasn't drunk. He was sat there, I insisted to myself, and the rush of adrenaline flooding my veins burned like the sweet sting of cold steel. I felt light-headed, and so I shut my eyes for a minute to shake it off.

"Merle!"

When I opened my eyes, he was gone. I wasn't seeing things. Wasn't imagining spectres. He was a bit worse for wear, shabby, frayed at the seams, but I would know those eyes anywhere. It *was* Jon.

"Merle!" I became vaguely aware that Henry was screaming my name, but he sounded distant, a mere echo in my mind. "Christ Merle, what the hell are ya doing there lass? You're bleeding," he said as he skidded on droplets that had fallen to mix with the spilled beer on the floor. "Bleeding all over the damn place, too!"

Henry grabbed my arm then a towel as he urgently and discreetly ushered me away from the bar.

It wasn't the first time I had cut too deeply, but I

was really trying to keep that little habit in check. I had become first-rate at the art of subtlety, and more often than not, I was able to pull it off as accidental, regardless of where I was. Henry knew better though. He gave me a scowl and shook me a bit. "Merle, I'm thinkin' you might want to run in the back and get yourself together. We've got people stickin' their nosey eyes to us now."

I was having trouble retrieving my head from my arse, so Henry paused for a moment, spun me around, and then shoved me towards the back room, whinging all the while. "We aren't runnin' a sideshow lassie, so for shite sake, go on with ya now."

Henry had always taken a fatherly tone with me, but it never offended me in the least. I knew in my heart that he was the only person in the whole of the world who actually cared about me. I felt the need to say I was sorry to him but couldn't muster enough humble to get it out, so I made my way to the toilets, head low, but no worse for the humiliation.

A little splash of cold water on my face, a proper bandage, and just that easy, I would be right as rain.

As I stood there, still of breath in front of the mirror, I noticed the bulb flickering fitfully above the washbasin. I should have replaced it a week ago. Should have done a lot of things, but again, I just stood there and stared at my reflection in the mirror as the cool water trickled over the wound and then swept down, swirling and spiralling the blood into the drain. It was a fleeting relief when the wound opened and the blood came, as if the poison were draining out of me. The pain wasn't so bad either, no more than a sting really, and it was remarkably better than what I felt inside. I don't know if I can describe it in words, and if I say sublime, you will really think I am a nutter.

However, my sanity is not up for debate.

Walking back towards the bar, I noted an excessive amount of people gathered around the men's toilets—up to no damn good I imagined—and as I got closer to the doorway, it became obvious that my imagining was probably correct: something was just not right.

A quick glance over the room confirmed that my pool-playing criminals were nowhere to be found, so I made a short detour to the back storage room in order to retrieve the other shotgun. I chambered the shells and then proceeded down the hallway.

Heart pounding, the smell of gun oil and blood on my hands, the only thought I had was of getting into the fray, and that thought gave me unadulterated delight.

3

Close Call

S tanding in front of the men's toilets, I took one deep breath before I kicked the door open. There wasn't time to think about the shaking in my arms or the unsteadiness of my legs. There was only time for instinct and madness, so I lifted the shotgun and took aim at the first thing that stirred in my rather wobbly line of sight.

Jonathan ... his name tormented my thoughts in drips of sticky heat running down the length of my arm to my elbow as I tried to process the moment before me. A familiar moment. A black moment. Fluorescent lights flickering. Taps dripping. The sickly scent of urine hanging in the air, and a crippled figure in agony, writhing round on the floor whilst six or so scummers beat him with pool cues, fists, and feet.

"Henry…" I screamed, but I wasn't entirely sure the words came out. The blunt, thudding echoes of fists against flesh seemed to absorb and deaden all sound, but I kept my calm … and my aim. "Lads, you know how I despise cleaning bloody toilets."

Sarcasm was my forte, and they all turned towards me and snickered in amusement. It was the best I could hope for, and at least the bludgeoning had stopped.

"HENRY," I screamed again as he came up behind me, chambering his rounds.

"I got yer back Lass, no worries." His response was that of a calm father, which was very reassuring and very much needed at that exact moment, so, since we seemed to have secured the lynch mob's undivided attention, I continued airing my objections with as much tact as one might bestow upon attempted murderers. "I am asking nicely now lads, move away from him and leave the premises straight away before I take a strong inkling to blowing someone's fuckin' face off."

They knew I wasn't fooling around. I not only had the minerals to point a gun at someone, I had the minerals to pull the trigger as well. That's the nice thing about everyone in the village knowing you're a little astray in the head: when you make arbitrary threats, they think twice. When you make threats with a weapon pointed at them, they tend to take you very seriously. Seriously enough to whinge about it, anyway.

There were brash mumblings from the group: "Mick will be pissed." "He was cheating." "Fuckin' thief." Typical accusations and an artful plethora of curse words, even for these idiots. They were just words, though. I've heard a lot of words over the years. Words mean very little in a world of actions and consequences. The man on the floor spoke no words, not even a whispered plea for mercy. He just lay there, dazed, bloody, a dishevelled wreck, arms covering his face and head like a shy schoolboy who'd just swatted a hornet's nest. Everything around me, in that moment, seemed insignificant compared to what I was feeling for him. I felt bad or was it sad? That stabbing in my stomach—damn it—I didn't know what I was feeling, except guilt.

Henry escorted the rest of the folks out, and in light of the circumstances, had decided—with much protest from the patronage—to close the pub early. It was either that or call the Garda. When Henry made up his mind about something, that was it. Nothing just short of a cattle prod could change it. Henry is, after all, the personification of stubborn old Irishman.

I helped the battered stranger up onto his feet, positioned his left arm over my shoulder, hoisted him up a bit, and led him out of the toilets. Weakened from the ordeal, he rested the full weight of his body against me a bit more intimately than I'm sure he was aware.

He was tall, yet thin, and easily manageable, and so I had little difficulty manoeuvring him about. Despite his awkwardness, and my unease, righting him seemed effortless, except that there was just something familiar about him, something odd that made me feel odd. The way he smelled. The way my arm felt around his waist. I shouldn't have been entertaining ideas, but the smell of blood and sweat on his clothes was morbidly arousing. Fanciful thoughts sped through my mind. I thought of the cliffs and the wildflowers. I thought of two bodies bared in the rain, so I looked away to hide a smile. It had been so long since I'd smiled, about anything, and that made me smile more until Henry's rude and incessant nitpicking, which managed to extricate that smile from my face instantly.

Stern and overly cautious reservations made Henry the old curmudgeon that he was, generally endearing, but right then, I didn't really want to hear it, so I suggested that he manage the lock up of the pub alone whilst I tended to our reluctant guest. He couldn't seem to extricate himself from my buts and what-ifs, so he huffed off, jangling the keys and waiving his fists over his head.

Good judgment isn't one of my strong suits, and I had a habit of picking up strays. Henry always said, "One of these days..." and one of these days, I might agree with him.

One of these days it could be a thief, or a rapist, or a homicidal maniac. Poor Henry, he had no idea I had one of those in my life already.

4

Wounds

I have a flat right over the pub. It's small, pleasant, and comfortable. Some might say shabby, but I like the words quaint and rustic. It suits my minimal needs, and it is my rather modest home. My father had wanted me to stay with him at his cottage when I arrived from abroad, but he knew that I was too independent to have a discussion about it, which would have inevitably turned into an argument, so he converted the dusty, second floor storage space into proper lodgings for me.

We often had arguments about what was best and what I should do, and I was sure if he could see me now, we'd be having a heated argument at that. His gentle suggestions chaffed in ways only a headstrong daughter would understand. Hurtful. Like he didn't believe in me. Like I couldn't take care of myself. I could. I just couldn't take care of other people, no matter how hard I tried.

I held the stranger tightly as we navigated up the darkened stairs into the sitting room, which was dimly lit by a tall, twisted, wrought iron lamp sat solitary in the corner of the room. I wasn't much for décor either.

"Sit down over there and take off your shirt," I said as I gestured towards the sofa with my hand and a smile that was probably more toothy than I had wanted it to be, so I feared for an instant that I might have said 'sit down' more instructionally than I had wanted to. *Please sit down.* That's what I'd wanted to say. I'd forgotten to be polite. I was, as a rule, more articulate than that, but he was just so beautiful that I was having difficulty unscrambling my brain enough to speak.

I switched on the brighter floor lamp next to the sofa and took a good long look at him.

"I have a first aid kit in the back," I explained. "Every good pub owner needs to know how to do a little triage, not to mention a shotgun rescue. Just another service we are happy to provide."

He smiled, reluctantly, looking down at his feet at the almost imperceptible dirt on the floor whilst I retrieved and assembled my makeshift hospital. Gauze, adhesive bandages, iodine, needle and thread. The only trouble was all the blood. Too much blood. I was feeling a little short of breath as other bloody moments tried to push themselves to the forefront of my mind. I had to fight for concentration, so in an attempt to refocus and forestall the panic attack I was about to have, I decided to take a detailed inventory of his beauty.

He could have been Jonathan's twin. The differences were so eerily subtle as to be insignificant at best. He was bristly, his face unshaved, but purposefully so, dark hair, like Jonathan's, but longer, hitting softly just at his shoulders and a whisper into his eyes. I don't even know where to begin with those eyes. They were exquisite. You could see through them straight to eternity—and blue—pale blue coloured eyes, as if he had stolen a bit of sky from heaven. I was completely captivated, and that was more than enough to stop my hands shaking.

"This one is quite deep and will need stitches," I said as I wiped the blood-soaked hair from his forehead. "I can stitch it, but it's going to hurt, and I think we should be properly introduced before I stick the needle to you."

"Lain," he replied in a deep velvety voice. "Why are you being so nice to me?"

"Well, Lain, you remind me of someone I adore. My name is Merle O'Byrne, and it's nice to meet you."

He winced as I made the first stitch.

Six in sum it took to close the wound, and with the blood washed away, he looked like nothing more than a bit of rough road. The bruises on his sides and abdomen were beginning to come to the surface, deep purple sludge coagulating under the skin, but nothing fatal, I assumed. I tended to assume a lot of things in life, but in reality, my assumptions were more wishes and prayers, except when I assumed things were my fault.

As I was packing up the first aid kit, he gave me a start with a look of hopefulness and gratitude, which had suddenly and uncomfortably arranged itself on his face out of nowhere. Hopefulness and gratitude are two things I never assume. I felt a little troubled by it, so to ease the dull thudding in my head, I reflexively rattled off a laundry list of calm-inducing instructions, "I am going to draw you a salt bath, Lain. Those bruises are coming in fast, and we don't want the blood to pool up too much. I think you have one or two cracked ribs as well. You can take as much time as you need. I am sure I have some clean clothes that will fit you."

That was all I could manage in one breath, so I felt it best to quit, seeing that I had the good sense to do so.

Whilst I ran the bath, he sat on the toilet, staring at the floor like a small, embarrassed child, and I felt a burgeoning sense of pity shift its weight. I don't think I had felt pity in ages; things had gotten so cold for me.

"Do you have anything to smoke?" he asked.

"Yes I do. I will bring some back and a shot of whiskey as well … might do you some good."

I turned off the water, grabbed a towel to dry my hands, and he got to his feet, just barely.

Fumbling with my thoughts, and the towel, I wondered which was worse, the physical or the emotional pain he felt as he struggled to be free of his trousers. I couldn't seem to work it out any more than I could get my hands dry without rubbing my skin off. I used to be more intuitive with people, but I'd lost confidence in that ability a long time ago. Had I been better at it, I might have been able to save Jonathan. No sense fretting over a lack of foresight, though. It's all shite an' bloody water under the fuckin' bridge now.

I left the room, closing the door slowly behind me.

After a moment in the darkened hallway, I went off rummaging for a pack of cigarettes and a bottle of *Jameson*. When I returned, the steam from the bath had completely clouded the small hallway, and as I neared the door, I could see him, naked in front of the mirror.

He was much worse off than I had realised. The welts were large, covering more than half of his body, and some were weeping fluid down his legs. He looked as if he hadn't had a decent meal in ages either. Tears welled up in my eyes, and I had a choking feeling in my chest. I turned my back to the door and cleared my throat to gain some composure, for the both of us.

He was in the bath when I entered the room.

"I'll just leave the bottle then," I said, averting my gaze for his comfort.

He did his best for a smile, so I left him, and then I set off determined to gather some clothes for him. I assumed he would fit in Jonathan's, as he had the same lanky build.

I hadn't touched Jonathan's wardrobe since picking out a suit for his funeral. Everything smelled musty, like graveyard dirt and stale cigarettes. As I was flinging garments about the room, a thought came to me: I never really understood why I hadn't gotten rid of Jon's things, or why I hadn't had a cigarette since the night he died yet I kept packs of his brand all over the flat. I guess right then, it all seemed so convenient that I hadn't completely purged him from my world, so I wrote it off to another one of those great mysteries of the universe. I always said the universe would provide the things you need when you need them. I've said a lot of crap things.

I made my way to the sitting room, sat myself down, lit a smoke, and closed my eyes. I was just so exhausted. My skin felt stretched and dry over my bones.

Determination is tiring, and I must have fallen asleep, I don't know for how long, but when I opened my eyes, I had the most enigmatic feeling of peace. Lain was stood in front of me, all dressed up proper in Jonathan's sunny weekend clothes. If it weren't for the stinging pain in my arm, I would have believed that I had died myself and was meeting my beloved in heaven. Too bad the feeling couldn't last. I doubted that heaven looked even remotely like my shabby flat, anyway, and a sense of gloom came over me as that realisation, and the pain in my arm, instantly delivered me back to the crap reality that was my life.

"Whiskey?" he asked, leaning in to hand me the bottle, and in spite of my muddled signals, he made no attempt to hide his solicitous tack. "We should probably take a look at your arm as well, it looks pretty bad."

I wanted to say, yes, wanted to admit that I, too, needed help, but for all his kindness, that wall of darkness crept in around me again ... and it was suffocating.

"My arm is fine," I shot back as I tucked it against my chest under the other. "You need to rest so take the spare room. I have a few things to tend to in the pub. I might be a couple of hours, and for your safety, I would strongly advise you to just stay put for the night."

I hadn't meant to be so curt, but it was too late to take the tone back. Besides, I didn't want the new chink in my armour to be so apparent anyway.

I got up and went down to the pub, leaving him stood there with the bottle of whiskey in his hand and a pathetic look of frustration trying to figure out how to fit itself onto his swollen face.

The pub was empty and quiet, so I sat at the bar, sipping my whiskey with a great deal of fortitude. Drinkers always think the drink will help relax them, give them confidence, take the edge off. It doesn't help. It never helps, except if you are trying to forget. With enough drink, you do forget, for a time, but then when you regain consciousness, the memories all come flooding back.

After we'd married, Jon moved in, and we made the upstairs flat our temporary marital home, and even though he rose early for his day job, he somehow managed to take on the pub with me as well, clean-up and all. I got the impression, on occasion, that although he liked accounting and it suited him, he would rather have been somewhere else doing something else.

That unsatisfied sense of longing was probably why Jonathan had always loved closing time. For a brief moment, the pub would become our own grimy paradise of sorts. Just the two of us. Blasting the music as loud as we could, all our cares lost to the wind, or rather, all our cares lost in the cracks and crevices, in the dust, ash, and in the backwash.

Every night would begin with Jon punching exactly the same songs up on the jukebox. I never really understood why he fancied those melancholy love songs so much, but we couldn't get through an evening without them. Since his death, I thought the songs reflected his idealised view of our love and the life less ordinary he had intended for us. Whatever anguish he felt, he took it with him to the grave. No one would ever know what those songs meant to him now, or if they brought him any joy at all. He never tapped his feet to the beat of the drums. Had never been much of a dancer, either, aside from the occasional Irish jig when he was pissed to the wind. He was simply too self-conscious for public displays of affection or bohemian carefree happiness. He kept his emotions close, preferring no outward show for fear that they might be misconstrued in some way.

I like to dance. Misconstrued intentions were not a worry for me. To cavort carelessly with the music gives me such a sense of freedom. He knew this and made a very valiant attempt for my benefit. We'd often pretend that we knew how to ballroom dance, feet sweeping concentric circles into the dusty grit on the floor, his one hand in mine, the other at my waist as our bodies cut through the stale air. I do like to dance. I loved to dance with him, but I knew he much preferred taking his pleasure watching me, even if he felt a little shameful in doing so. He often said he felt sterile and wished he were more free spirited like I was. I, of course, reassured him that I loved him exactly the way he was.

That was the truth. I did and still do.

So, every evening, once Henry left for the night, I would snatch a moment to myself, play Jon's favourite songs, and, in what seemed like a lifetime of small agonizing moments, I would dance as if it were the very last moment I would ever know.

Sometimes I wished it were, and other times, I was hopelessly unaware of how close I was to the end.

5

I Dreamt *of a Monster*

D idn't see it coming. The hard smack. The blinding pain. The metallic taste in my mouth. I crumpled to the floor as his shadow fell against the light, looming over me, filling me up with blackness and dread. "I think you've been ignoring me lassie, and rumour on the street is that you're hiding a fugitive from me."

"Nice to see you too, Mick..." I spat a mouthful of blood onto his shoes for spite, and as I struggled to get to my feet, I couldn't help but ask, "...and what in the fuck are you getting on about?"

It was a right stupid question, and apparently, my duplicity was not appreciated. He grabbed me, hauled me up, and slammed me against the wall. I kept my eyes closed, and even though I couldn't see his, I could feel the cruelty, in his voice, in the hot stench of his breath on my neck. Could taste it in the air around me. He tasted like the stinking carcass of a rabid animal.

"You know you're my whore, and whores should know their place, shouldn't they, Merle?"

I didn't answer.

"The lads tell me that you distracted them whilst they were trying to work tonight. You know I don't like distractions, Merle. I don't like unfinished business either, and right now, I'm finding it difficult to like you. I know you want me to like you, Merle. Yes you do."

I ignored his words and looked him dead in the eyes, cold black eyes that mirrored the ugliness of the world, but I wasn't afraid of that blackness. I had been there before, in suffocating madness, so nothing he might say or do could ever really harm me.

"Your dogs need to mark their territory somewhere else, Mick," I replied. "I know what you're *really* here for. So, are we going to do this thing or what?"

There was no real need for an answer to that question. He sucked the dribble of saliva off his lower lip, grinned, thrust his hand into my hair, and then dragged me off to the toilets.

Mick had been Jon's best mate at university. The details of the introduction are sketchy and riddled with grey areas and inconsistencies. Mick wasn't even a student there. All I really know about that moment in Jon's life is that he was by-the-book studious straight and narrow, and Mick, well, Mick was always looking for a shortcut. Mick envisioned a fortune in drugs and petty crime. No one stood in his way, and he was relentless and cruel as if he were wholly aware that he had no soul.

He was responsible for Jon's death. Even though he would never outwardly admit it, I was convinced of that.

He enjoyed the power. Enjoyed pushing people over the edge. It was sport for him, a twisted game that he loved playing, and I loved never giving him the satisfaction he desired. He would never declare victory over me.

Never.

He was the embodiment of my nightmares, the monster that took my beloved, and for what it's worth, he was my penance.

The frequency of his violations had diminished over the years. Maybe he was getting bored, or maybe the debt Jon owed to him had finally been paid off. He rarely beat me anymore. Being able to admire the scars he'd previously gifted me seemed to be enough for him. I never knew why he chose to show me mercy in any given moment, if that's what it was. Didn't much care to know either.

The moments with Mick were not as sharp as they used to be, not as comforting as I needed them to be. He was nothing more than a coward, so it was nothing more than a dull aching at best, and it barely muffled my own pain any longer. In the end, all that lingered of him was a feeling of sadness and a filth I couldn't wash off.

I expected he would leave me or kill me someday, and I was hoping for the latter.

I squeezed my eyes closed tight and tried to picture Jon until it was over.

Neither a tear nor a whimper had I ever given.

6

Confessions *in a Cup of Coffee*

I t was about half-four in the morning as I crept back up to the flat. Lain seemed to be deep in a fitful sleep, and I'd hoped that the steam from the shower wouldn't wake him. The fog had cleared from my head, and I only wanted to wash off the evil and crawl into bed. I always slept as if I had somehow achieved redemption with Mick, but that feeling never lasted long enough to make a damn bit of difference. By morning, the anguish would have returned in all its searing intensity. This moment, this morning, it didn't though. It couldn't put its chokehold on me because it's amazing how much better someone can look after a decent cup of coffee and a hot meal. The lavender scented steam had woken Lain. He was already in the kitchen by the time I stumbled in, robe askew, hair up in a towel. He winced at me instead of what I thought should have been a smile. He was still in quite a bit of pain made obvious by the stiffness of his body and his demeanour. Yet his battered appearance did not detract from his beauty in any way. Now that it was daylight, I could make a thorough assessment of the damage done to him. He would heal, but it was going to take some time—time I secretly hoped in my heart would be with here, with me.

"I am sorry I was short with you last night," I said as I filled his coffee cup again. "It wasn't your fault. I was having a troublesome night."

He took a sip of his coffee and then looked over his cup with questioning eyes. "Was it the man who came in late last night?"

"Were you spying on me, Lain?"

"No, no I wasn't. I heard a voice, that's all. I'm sorry. Is he a mate?"

I was taken aback slightly by the question, and I was sure that my tone would lilt towards irritation when I finally got around to answering. There are a lot of endearments and expletives that one might use when describing the people in your life. Mate was not one of the words I would choose to use whilst describing Mick.

I lit a cigarette and sat down at the table.

"Mick isn't a mate to anyone, Lain. His bulldogs were the fellows who were having their way with you last night. I don't mean to lecture you, but it's generally not a good idea to walk into a village and mix it up with the locals when you have no idea who the dangerous ones are. It's a good way to get yourself killed. Do you understand?"

I could see that he was working something out in his head. He, too, lit a cigarette, put his coffee down, and then came the question I knew he was going to ask, "How are you involved with him then? Your husband?"

It took me a moment to catch my breath, and when I did, I choked out the reply, trying to keep my temper under control, "First Lain, you don't know me well enough to ask these sorts of questions. Second, you must already know about my husband, or you wouldn't have that craptastic look slapped all over your face, and third, to answer your question: yes. Mick was my husband's best mate, and I say *was* because my husband Jon was lousy at choosing his mates. My husband is DEAD. He lost his bloody mind, and he blew his fuckin' brains out downstairs in the toilets, the very same toilets with which you yourself are intimately familiar. Sad. Tragic. Unfortunate. I hear it all the time: poor Merle, her dead husband, and her sad, tragic, and unfortunate situation. That's about as much of a story as there is to tell, so it's best not to ask any more questions about Mick."

I stormed out of the room before he could fumble with an apology. Who did he think he was anyway? Just look at the state of him. How dare he pity me.

7

The Abyss *in the Barrel of a Gun*

There was a small section of the attic that my father had left idle and unfinished. Actually, convinced that it was useless for any purpose other than an aviary for bats, he ignored it. An absurdly narrow and creaky set of stairs, hidden behind the panelling in the far corner of the master bedroom, gave access. Cobwebs hung in the corners, crisp winds whistled through the eaves, and the small gabled window, built into the steep peak of the roof, let in the evening light. When the sunset cast its ruddy glow on the open beams, it made the room seem on fire.

I absolutely loved that little secret room.

It was our secret kissing room.

At weekends, Jon and I would hide from my father during the afternoon lunch rush. It was easy to just go missing when the pub was crowded and busy. I couldn't stop giggling as we stole up the stairs, and Jon would always crinkle his brows, put his finger to his lips, and whisper, "Merle, sshhh."

We would hide in that little closet of a room and kiss for hours. I could have spent an eternity kissing Jon—no words—we spoke only in breath.

The memory makes my soul shiver still.

It was my favourite room. My darkness, my innocence, and my passion locked within it.

Shortly after his death, I turned the kissing room into a shrine for him. I filled the room with all of the things he cherished: his favourite books by Gibran and Kafka, his collection of sad love songs, his favourite tweed jacket that still smelled of his aftershave if I inhaled deeply enough, and his delicate wire-rimmed glasses, which complimented his bookish good looks.

The photo collage I had assembled on the walls was a brilliant allegorical work of art, in my opinion. It amounted to painstaking years of effort. Every fibre of my being had gone into it, and I loved its eloquent representation of his every mood, subtle as they were. Sometimes when I stared at those pictures, I thought I could see a darkness in his eyes that I hadn't noticed in all the time we were together.

It was my fault.

I hadn't been paying close enough attention.

I failed him.

As I sat alone in our room, I found myself clutching the pistol Jon had purchased for me when we first met. He had said that he didn't feel safe leaving me alone at the pub without something with which to protect myself, should the necessity arise. This was altogether out of character for Jon. He hated violence, but he had felt some deep-seated need to give it to me, and I wasn't about to say no. It was a beautifully ornate old-fashioned pistol. Jonathan said it was like something out of the old gypsy movies, and he thought that it suited me—sparkling and dangerous.

Was that how he saw me?

I probably wasn't, but *it* was dangerous. Gravely so. It hadn't been fired until the night he died, and it hadn't been fired since, despite my best efforts.

I kept it cleaned, polished, and with one round always in the cylinder. I liked to think of it as the round that shattered our marriage. An antiques dealer Jon worked with knew a smithy, who in turn made the bullet for me. A unique bullet, made from the finest metal ever forged—our wedding rings—and I'd had our names engraved upon it, in loving memory. I know it seems twisted, to be so fixated on death, but I believed that if I had the bullet with my name on it, maybe, just maybe, I would have more control over my destiny. It was a fuckin' ridiculous idea, obsessive even, but knowing that bullet was in there gave me some small sense of comfort. It probably wouldn't even fire, but it was comforting to try. I spun the cylinder, took a deep breath, and brought the gun to my head…

I liked the coldness of the steel pressing into me, I liked the way all of the silence in the world filled the room, and I liked that I felt contented, as if death had wrapped its cloak around me to keep me from shivering in the dark.

…Click.

I exhaled.

Not today, then.

I let the pistol drop to the floor, and I wept.

I wept a depthless sorrow. I would give anything for

the wet of his lips, the soft touch of his hands, and the sweetness of his voice again. I didn't think I could endure the torment any longer. Didn't think I could ever be satisfied with my punishment. I'd painted myself red with hatred, with love, with despair and denial, but the only thing I could ever seem to do with any of that was weep, and I don't even know how long I did that before I fell asleep. Don't know how long I'd slept, either, but it must have been getting late, because the evening fire was just kindling in the window.

Henry would be wondering where I was, and...

I expected that my stranger would be gone since I had put him off so rudely. Who would blame him?

Stumbling over myself in my haste, I ran down the stairs and flung my body across the hall into the bathroom. I splashed some cold water on my face, changed out of my guilt-soaked clothes, and headed to the kitchen for a much-needed cup of tea. It was all too much in twenty-four hours. I would drink my tea and get back to some normalcy, though I had no idea what normal was anymore.

I was shocked and deeply pleased to find Lain in the kitchen, kettle in hand. He smiled at me, and I think I actually blushed.

"I'm sorry," he said as he handed me a cup of tea. "You were so nice to me, and I only wanted to talk with you. I should have been more careful with my choice of questions. I didn't mean to upset you, and I didn't want to leave without telling you that. I'll drink my tea, and then I'll be on my way."

I don't how he did it. This time he looked like a scolded child, and I felt my chest tighten. I felt that pity I'd had for him change into something else, something warm, something I hadn't felt in a long time.

"No," I said, "I'm the one who was rude. It's a difficult subject for me to talk about, and last night's goings-on didn't help matters. Too much excitement to keep a clear head." I sat down, lit a smoke, sipped my tea, and continued, "I think you need a little more time to heal those injuries, and you don't seem to be carrying around much in the way of baggage. I'm going to be forward here, OK? The fact is, Henry, the stiff old bloke downstairs, isn't getting any younger, and the long nights are becoming difficult for him. I could use some help around the pub, and it would be nice to have the company. I can pay you a regular wage, with room and board of course. You know, just until you feel better and are on your feet again. What do you think?"

You would have thought I'd held my breath for hours waiting for his reply.

He looked up over his cup, smiled, and I let out an embarrassing sigh of relief. Then we both laughed.

It was nice to laugh.

8

Echoes *in the Rain*

S everal weeks passed without incident. Lain said that he was feeling well, and he had really taken a shine to working the pub. If it needed doing, Lain did it. Henry had even started to warm up to him and was appreciating the freedom to retire early without fretting about me all night. Though Henry's fretting was the least of my worries, because of late, a simple walk along the streets had become an adventure in nobody minding their own business. The village knitting Nellies were buzzing about the *stranger* at Merle's, and considering the oral traditions of the village—oral fixations, rather—it didn't take long for the hearsay to wind its way around the entire countryside: Who was he? Where did he come from? And, of course, since he stayed with me, everyone wanted to know if we were sleeping together, as if sex would fix all of my problems.

Hardly.

But that's the thing about small villages: you can't keep anything secret. Anything worth knowing will be known to everyone eventually, so it's best not to know anything in the first place. I never asked Lain any questions. I figured that if he wanted me to know something he would offer the information of his own free will. He showed me the same courtesy. Most of the time we just shared an uneasy yet respectful silence, until a night came when silence wouldn't be an option.

That night did come, like I knew it would, and it was a particularly savage night in the middle of May. The rain was coming down in stinging swaths that felt like shrapnel when it hit your skin. We needed pub supplies, and Henry was the one who, on most occasions, went into the city centre to get what we needed. The weather, being as dreadful as it was, created concern for Henry's safety. His eyesight was failing and so were his reflexes. It was a long winding drive through the middle of nowhere, so Lain offered to go instead. The routine was to leave right before close and be back with the supplies by late morning next day.

I had that sick stabbing feeling in my stomach again. I feared he would not return. Being the waif that he was, I had wondered often over the past few months when his last day would come. We all have a day where we decide we don't want to be where we are. Some have more of those days than others do. I tried not to look directly at him as I handed him the keys to the lorry. I didn't want him to see the fear in my eyes.

He did anyway.

"No worries, Merle." He smiled and plucked my chin before setting off on his way.

Over the course of the evening, I tried not to consider my non-worries. I considered the maleficent weather. I considered that the night seemed slow to the point of being endless, so Henry and I considered a couple of pints for ourselves while we chatted on late into the wee hours. Henry could spin a yarn for sure, and I always welcomed listening to tales about my father. My father was a burly virile man, well respected, "a man not above himself," Henry said. Raising a daughter on his own, especially one as wilful as I was, had to be difficult for someone who was always concerned about outward appearances. Nevertheless, the staunch disciplinarian had a bit of wild in his eye. He taught me to free my heart and my mind, taught me to be unconventional, and to show no mercy when I felt bound. I don't think I could have survived without his lessons. I miss him so. He was the only honest man I'd ever loved.

Henry and my father had been childhood best mates, typical rowdy Irish lads tearing up the village. They favoured each other in manner and spirit, although I felt that Henry was a softer, lighter version.

Neither of their lives turned out as they had yearned for and intended. The harsh realities were mortally wounding. My father had fallen in love with an astonishingly beautiful tourist, "painfully beautiful," he often said of her. She was lustrous at twenty-one, vibrant, committed to freedom and the countryside. My father fell hard and fast. He followed her back to the States where they wed straight away. I arrived shortly thereafter. But my mother's spirit could not be tamed. She was a selfish woman, wanting more than a hard-working immigrant man could provide. She wanted adventure and cosmopolitan intrigue, so much so that she disappeared when I was five, never to return. My father was a man without a home, a country, and a heart. He mourned the loss of her eternally.

Henry's life wasn't any easier. He'd married his childhood sweetheart only to lose her and his baby daughter in childbirth three years later. Henry's parents had passed on at a young age, and his wife's parents shunned him. It was as if they felt that his desire had killed not only their beloved child but their dreams of immortality as well. He had no one to turn to.

When my heartsick father finally found the means to return from abroad, they clung to each other like long-lost brothers bound by sorrow. Two impetuous old curmudgeons. Pillars of the community, and a mighty force to be reckoned with. In certain circles, it was said that they, "ran things 'round the place." My father got things done that needed doing for anyone in the village who asked for his help, and he did it without fuss, though Henry loved to exaggerate my father's escapades. Each story was appropriately festooned with waving arms, scowls, hair-raising melodrama, and carnival-barker quality narrations. Henry loved my father as much as I did, and that was no exaggeration.

By the time my father rang me in the States and asked me to take over the family business, he was already very ill, a significant detail both he and Henry had kept hidden from me for quite some time. It wasn't a difficult deception since there was a sea and a whole world between us. I forgave them both for the lie. But Henry was good at keeping secrets, for he had also promised my father that he would look after me until the end of his own days. Being proud and independent, I would have been mortified had I known of that promise initially. Now I am grateful. Uncle Henry, since the day my father passed, he had never left my side.

Anyway, Henry and I had considered a few too many pints. He was pissed and had decided to stay with me for the night. I had no objections to his decision since I hadn't been alone in months, and I wasn't particularly fond of the idea anymore, so I went up to the flat in order to set up the spare cot and put the kettle on for tea.

I find time seems to stand still on rainy nights, but as I stood in the kitchen setting out the tea and biscuits, I became very aware of the silence *and* the time. An awfully long amount of time had passed, and Henry had not come up from the pub yet. So I turned the cooker off and went off to collect him.

Maybe he had fallen asleep in the back room: he sometimes did that during the day. On my way, I noticed the overhead lights were on, and the ashtrays along the bar top were still filthy. Henry would never overlook those trifling details unless he was totally soused. As I headed for the back room, I saw a figure move in the darkness. Had he not heard me calling him?

"Henry."

I was about to call out again when the shadows broke in front of me, and the creature that stepped out of that inky darkness, I knew all too well. I didn't feel a thing. Everything went black, and I was overcome with a slow floating feeling, as if I were drifting backwards. I rolled over onto my back, but for all the blood in my eyes, I could just barely see Mick stood over me— smiling. When I came to, my hands were bound.

"Ah, you're awake now luv," he said in his revoltingly sarcastic way of speaking. "Sorry I had to pistol whip you, but you just piss me all the way off. Your boyfriend being here all the time has really cramped my style, but we are going to get some things straight tonight, aren't we now, Merle?"

I loathed him so intensely.

I wanted to stab him in the eyes.

I wanted to scream but could only manage to whisper, "Where's Henry?"

"He's taking a little nap luv ... don't worry, he won't be botherin' us for a while."

He seized my wrists and hoisted me up over the side of the pool table. I knew what was going to happen next, but I was so worried about Henry that my situation seemed to matter little, so I resigned myself, considered myself, and then convinced myself that it was just an unpleasant ordeal as I took a deep breath, as I felt the back of my shirt cut loose from me.

Mick tossed the fabric aside and then thrust the blade into the pool table right next to my head. My own hunting knife, how humiliating, and he revelled in my humiliation. Grabbing a fistful of my hair, he leant into my ear, his hot breath on my neck as he whispered, "Now don't move on me, or that goes in your neck."

I could feel spittle running down my face, could smell his sweat mixed with chalk dust and stale whiskey. I was going to vomit, and as the sick filled my mouth, I could faintly hear the buckle of his belt coming undone. The snap of the leather. There was no escaping my fate, but I deserved it and wanted no release from it.

The first strike was always the hardest to take. Bolts of lightning shooting through my veins, and there would be many more. He wouldn't have his way until I was good and bloody. He preferred it that way, and I preferred not to acknowledge that fact, so thankfully, the dizziness comes quickly—that luxurious light feeling that makes you forget what's happening and all the moments within moments that happened before it. I wanted that so much, might have even begged for it, but it was a luxury I could not afford. I needed to stay strong. I needed to hold on to my sanity through the pain. Just. Hold. On. But reality has a blinding fury to it, a searing sarcasm. I wasn't sure if my mind was playing tricks on me when I thought I heard a faint clicking sound through the screaming in my head and the rain.

"You sadistic fucker!"

It was Lain, just stood there, a shadow in a doorway, rain-soaked, shaking, with the barrels of a shotgun aimed directly at Mick's head, but Mick's expression didn't change. He turned to face Lain, shrugged it off, and laughed. "You're a mouthy cunt, ain't ya? What? You think because you look like her dead husband that you can come in here and take what doesn't belong to you. That's a fuckin' gas, ain't it?" He walked defiantly towards the door and spat in Lain's face. "We ain't through me and her. She ain't done paying her dead husband's due yet. Anyway, what do you care, gypo? You're just passin' through, right? Just a bloody nuisance and you look like a sloppy seconds sort of bloke. Besides," he said, "she wants it, and she likes it. I'm the best she's ever had."

Mick walked out the door into the rain with a "Go on, ask her," trailing off behind him, and Lain remained stood there, shaking, almost frozen in the moment, until the door slammed shut and the courageous façade that was keeping him upright crumbled in on him.

He couldn't have shot anyone, even if he had wanted to.

9

The Argument

Henry would need to remain in hospital for a few days. It was only a concussion, but due to his age, the doctors wanted to keep a cautious eye on him. I couldn't shake the chill that came with the thought of losing him, so Lain and I decided to return to the flat in order to get some rest. Rest is what I needed, not talk. I don't like heated discussions. I wasn't angry, but it was obvious that Lain was, just a bit. Angry that I had not been more forthcoming to the Garda about what had happened. Angry that I had asked him to keep his mouth shut. Silence. It was in everyone's best interest, and my sole concern was for Henry. Lain barely looked at me the entire drive back to the pub, and I felt his anger in an emptiness spreading out between us.

When we arrived home, I immediately put the kettle

on and took off my jacket and my hat. Even my hair hurt.

I lit a smoke.

When I looked up, Lain was leaning in the doorway to the kitchen with a look on his face I didn't care for — sullen and cold. "What?" I asked.

"Is this how it's going to be then, Merle?" He straightening his stance, arms still crossed. "Is it true and please don't turn your back on me; the kettle doesn't need fussing with. I just want to know. Is it true?"

"What do you mean?"

"Merle, come on. What he said, is it true?"

I knew exactly what he'd meant. I'd lied. I admit it, and I could feel his eyes, like hot steel pokers, penetrating the back of my head, but it's one thing to lie and another to be accused of being a liar. The last thing I ever expected was such a judgemental tone from him.

"What do you want me to say, Lain? That I *let* him do it to me. That I *enjoy* it. That he is the best I've ever had at tormenting me? At fucking me? Is that what you want to hear? A confession so you can get off on it. Poor Merle. You men ... you're all the same. Needing a woman to be crazy or weak."

I was screaming by this point or at least I thought that I was. I couldn't actually hear anything. Everything sounded like static, as if someone had tuned the world out of frequency.

"Yes, Lain, the answer is YES. I LET him do it to me. I fuckin' DESERVE it. He takes what he wants and it's nothing, because you see, Lain, there's NOTHING left to take..." I got right up into his face, and with all the contempt I could muster, I whispered, "...and every girl needs a bit of rough now and then."

I smiled at him, and he punched me so hard to the face that I lost my footing and fell backwards, slamming my head into the cupboard. I could feel and taste the blood trickling down the back of my throat. When I looked up at him, he was just stood there, arms crossed again, with his head cocked to the side.

The calmness in his face was frightening. Dead calm.

I was frightened, terrified in fact.

Merle, who'd taken everything Mick could dish out, who'd watched her husband and father die. Merle, who wasn't scared of a single thing in her life, was terrified. I slid, pulling myself across the kitchen floor towards the hallway, desperately stumbling to get to my feet.

"Oh now, Merle … where are ya going there, lass? We're needin' to finish our discussion, I think, and you might *not* want to be admittin' that last statement to just anyone."

I tried to get up, but he put his foot on my spine and pushed me back down to the floor. He was so calm when he told me that, "there was no sense fighting," before he lunged at me. He was so calm when he asked me if, "*this* was the way I wanted it," before he landed almost on top of me. And I struggled, violently. Kicking, twisting, punching. I wasn't even sure I was connecting with anything. I'd considered my fate, considered that one of these days might be today, and then I realized that there was little left for me to consider except survival. Survival is a dark savage thing to consider, and nothing makes any sense in the static but your anger.

How could this be happening?

Oh God Henry, you were right.

I am going to die.

When he got to his feet to make another lunge for me, I kicked his legs out from under his body, and he fell on top of me, which was advantageous … to him. Straddling me, he tried to pin my wrists to the floor in an effort to restrain my crazed flailing assault, but before he could secure my right, I felt my fist connect. Droplets of spit and blood sprayed my skin as his face moved closer to mine. I shut my eyes. I couldn't look at him. I was exhausted. I'd trusted him. He was the liar. A wolf in sheep's clothes, and I had no will left to fight the betrayal.

Was this how I wanted it?

Was it?

Did I enjoy being the victim?

Perhaps, and I was too much of a coward to admit it. Had I truly loved Jonathan? Am I even capable of loving anyone at all, or had I surrendered to the abyss—in love with the darkness I had found there?

"Merle!"

I'm no one, stood in the middle of nowhere. Screaming. I don't even know who I am, and there's all this screaming.

"Merle! Open your eyes."

My father's screaming. Henry's screaming. Jonathan's screaming, and Mick is just laughing.

The end of my reality, and I can't make a sound.

"Please fuckin' look at me, Merle!"

No armour, no wall, and no absolute blackness could hold them back any longer. Tears. I might not have been able to scream, but I could cry. I opened my eyes, and let a flood of hopelessness stream down my face as I looked straight into his—so blue—pale beautiful blue—stolen from heaven.

"Merle. Listen to me, damn it."

His voice echoed throughout the room. Unsteady and unsure as it pierced through the depths and the blackness, "I'm NOT Jon. I'm not that sick sadistic bastard either, and … and you're *not* who everyone thinks you are, Merle. You just got cornered."

And it was a very dark and small corner, in a very dark and small pit—one that I had dug myself—and if I was going to get out of it, I had to stop clawing at the walls and look up. Look up into the moonlight, an innocent sparkle in his eyes. Look up beyond the anger, sweet dewdrops on the wet of his lips. I wanted him. A desperate want that stank of sweat and fear. I was trembling. I wanted to tell him everything, but the words, the fear, it was all still there, as faint as a whisper caught in the darkness: *Is this what it means to be alive? To survive?* I don't know. Am I alive, but for my shadow and the darkness?

This pain, is it mine?

Quick and yet motionless,

Lit upon silken vapours as if it were a dream.

A dream once lost.

Rapturous it was once, this dream. My dream of him.

A dream of want clinging to commingled breath.

A dream of desire deepening.

A dream of he and me.

Of blood, of rage, of bared skin.

A dream with a will to hasten,

A dream lost, invariably, but not forsaken.

10

Decision *to Stay*

Considering my appearance, I had decided to keep the pub closed for a couple of days, at the very least until Henry was out of hospital. In truth, I think the real reason was that I didn't want to leave the comfort of Lain's embrace. We stayed in bed for a week straight, only emerging for tea and food.

I lost count of how many times we made love, each time in turn better than the last as we gained familiar comfort with each other. His touch was invigorating, frantic, and forceful, as if fuelling a hunger that wouldn't be satisfied. I wasn't used to this needfulness. Mick just took what he wanted, and Jon…

Jonathan had been an exceptionally gracious lover, precise, careful, deliberate, and generous to a fault. True to his nature, his passion was subdued, though. Guarded.

He had to allow you know him in order to feel him. Lain, on the other hand, had declared himself a simple man. Laissez-faire and straightforward. He never asked about Jon, but I got the feeling that he wanted to. We all compare ourselves to others even when we say we don't. I felt guilty enough that Jon was absent from my thoughts more often these days. Guilty that the feelings I had for Lain were beyond my control, so we never discussed our prior romantic or sexual relationships. It's that silence thing again, but we weren't mute. Henry was coming home, and we were planning to re-open the pub with a huge welcome home party. I had so much to do: decorations, cake, party favours, not to mention that the pub looked and smelled as if a scrapyard windstorm had done a bit of renovating. Chaos. I was so very excited just to get back to the chaos of life again, yank up the bootstraps, dust myself off, but a little selfish part of me didn't want to leave the cocoon I had wrapped myself into with Lain.

A sliver of sun shot through the clouds onto the bed. It flickered and danced like a mystical flame of approval from the heavens. We were meant to be. It just felt so perfect lying there, side by side, engulfed in the noonday's fire, and I was trying desperately to cling to the comfort of that moment. I hadn't felt anxious in a week, but with opening time on the horizon, I could feel it starting to crawl over my skin with every passing hour. Lain sensed my body stiffening as he stared at the wounds on my back. He put his hand on my shoulder, and so tenderly, he said, "No worries, Merle … alright?"

"Yes. No worries," I lied, again.

He didn't seem to notice the lie or care. He squeezed me tight, leant into my ear, and whispered comforts and ablutions, "He will never touch you again."

I knew he meant it, even if I didn't think he could commit to it, and so I rolled over to face him, kissed him on the lips. "Lain, can I ask you something?"

He nodded and kissed my forehead.

"Why did you come back that night? I know you wanted to leave, for good."

"I don't know, Merle. I had a feeling I guess, and, I'd forgotten my umbrella."

We made love until the opening.

11

Smiling Again

A summertime had swiftly come and gone since Henry's riotous welcome home party. The rest of the town was stuck in a deep layer of melancholia at the change of seasons, but not Henry. He pranced about the place fit-as-a-fiddle, his ornery old self. Time has a way of making space for the new, and a freshly minted sense of peace finally reigned over all. For me, that meant no accidents and no dark thoughts. No one ever mentioned that dreadful evening, either.

Henry had taken such a liking to Lain that they almost seemed like father and son. Whilst betting pints on pool games, they laughed and joked all through the night. They were a pure joy to behold. The two of them reminded me so much of my father and Jonathan that I was beginning to feel like part of a family again.

Lain never stopped talking either, just like Henry, and I never tired of listening to his life stories. He spoke of his mother, vaguely and briefly, and of the seemingly endless parade of abusive men who had, for a time, masqueraded as stepfathers. His mother gave up and died, he said, when he was only sixteen, of drinking and an immeasurable sadness, wrapped up in her own melodrama. He said that he felt nothing as he looked upon her corpse, nothing but the typical unaffecting bleakness of rainy winter's day. He had run away then, just after the funeral, with only the clothes on his back. He has been a waif ever since, taking odd jobs here and there for room and board.

Now that sort of freedom might seem like a dream: to go where you please, answer to no one, a bit of drifting stardust on the breeze, every day bringing with it the promise of new intrigues and adventure, but according to Lain, he had seen quite a bit of the world but never felt as though he belonged anywhere. Never felt wanted, needed, or part of any greater design.

No one, in the middle of nowhere.

I could relate as I had felt the same when I first came to this country. It was so foreign in a dramatic and dis-heartening sort of way, and the locals treated strangers as if they were plague carriers worse than rats. I only ever wanted to fit in and eventually call it my home, too. Even with father and Henry around, I still felt so hopelessly disoriented, but then Jon came along and changed everything for the better. He made this island feel like home, and after my father died, Jon was home. Without him, all I had left were the pub's stone walls, which mirrored the wall I had built around my heart. Strong, maybe, but remove a couple of stones from the foundation, and the whole thing falls apart.

Until now, those walls had insulated me, deadened my senses to life and all its misery. Until now. Now they were crumbling—crumbling at the feet of a stranger. A stranger who might have seemed odd and distant at first glance, when in reality, he was exceedingly easy to get on with. Just a mislaid kindred-spirit, and he understood my affectations, including my inability to open up with people. Lain was different. I never had any difficulty prattling on about my father, Henry, the pub, or my transient childhood growing up in the States, but even with Lain, my perfect stranger, I felt terribly uncomfortable talking about Jonathan. I thought that if I spoke of him offhandedly, he would become a caricature, or worse yet, disappear from my memory altogether. Lain often insisted that he needed to know everything about me, and that Jon was a part of that everything. I had to make a choice. I wasn't much for making choices, and Lain wasn't good at compromise. His insistence was non-negotiable, so I started at the beginning of the end, when Jon's career took a turn for the worse.

Redundancy they called it. It's humiliating to be labelled redundant, and Jon took that label to heart. He felt unworthy. That he wasn't going to be able to provide for me. The most fabulous life promise he had made on our wedding day weighed on him like a breezeblock tied to his neck. I didn't recall such a promise, but I attempted to console him with a bit of this and that. After all, we had the pub and my inheritance. I knew we were going to be all right, but I couldn't seem to convince him of that fact. He just grew more soul-stricken and despondent with each passing day.

Then, his 'ole mate' from university began lurking around the pub more often. There were whispered conversations, Jon's drinking increased, and he would go missing at all hours of the day and night. He was strung out. I could see it. In the dark circles under his eyes. The habitual silence. One evening, I found him crouched down in the kitchen, crying and shaking uncontrollably. He told me that he and Mick had gotten into some sort of gambling thing and that he had lost all of my father's money. He said he didn't deserve me, didn't deserve anything, and that I needed to let him go.

Of course, I refused. Letting him go was out of the question. Go where? The money meant nothing. My love for him and his love for me. Love. It was the only thing that meant anything at all to me. I was a part of him, he was a part of me, and we were part of something better than this. A gambling debt was insignificant in my opinion. Money comes and goes. It's there and then it's not. You struggle a bit, then you get past it. We'd figure it all out. I knew we would.

I held his trembling body until he fell asleep. My heart was breaking, and I didn't know what to do, or say, or feel for that matter. I kissed him gently, covered him with a blanket, and then decided a shower would help clear my head. I had no idea that he had taken the pistol until I heard the shot.

He had left a note on the table:

'You have to let me go. I love you. Jon.'

I spent the remainder of that night huddled against his body in blood-soaked sorrow.

In the aftermath of telling that story, I wept for hours, and Lain held me through it. He never said a word.

Other than the Garda, I had never told a single soul what had taken place that night. I had hoped with time and distraction that I would forget it, but I've discovered that time doesn't heal anything. You can ignore it, but you can't erase it, and distraction only replaces one kind of pain with another. It cancels itself out in the end. Everything does. It's tiring to have to work so hard to forget. Life is exhausting. Confessions are exhausting. Atonement is exhausting, so I fell asleep mid-breakdown because I didn't have the strength to choose anything else. When I awoke, I looked up to Lain, contentedly seated in the chair across from me, smoking a cigarette, just looking at me.

I love the way he looks at me.

"I want you to tell me something, Merle." He exhaled and leant forward, clasped his hands together. "I want you to tell me one memory you have of Jon that defines completely why you loved him."

"Why? What purpose could it possibly serve?"

"Merle, please, just do it."

It wasn't a difficult question to answer. My protest had nothing to do with that. It had everything to do with holding onto the hurt. Sure, I could offer up a thousand timid reminiscences that I long feared had been forgotten. I could do that, with a plaintive sigh. I could clear my throat, pretend to be gracious, or I could tell him that Jon had always accepted me. Simple as that. "You see, Lain, I was of the opinion that *lingerie* meant his old boxers and a t-shirt. I felt weird about the word sexy in a thousand different ways, always have, but all Jon could ever say to me, after he laughed at me, was that he liked weird. That he thought weird was sexy."

Lain smiled, nodded his head.

"Now you can let him go, Merle."

We never spoke of Jon again.

12

On the Subject *of Murder*

I t was coming up on the end of October. Dark, brisk nights. The smell of crushed flowers and fallen leaves, bonfire embers dancing in the air as the moon leant lower against the horizon. All Hallows was upon us. The veil was thin, and I could sense the spirits more than usual. Lain attempted to interject some calm by saying that it was just my imagination. Shadows and wind in the eaves. I certainly wanted to believe that, and so I brushed off the dread as best I could.

Lain and I had settled into the business of pub ownership quite nicely, and since we were considered a couple by the village sewing circle, I compensated him as a partner instead of an employee. Of course, that payment was generally taken out in trade.

Henry had officially declared himself retired, and so

he frequented the pub purely for his own enjoyment, which was frequently more and more frequent. I don't think we could have done without his tall tales for long anyway. All was right with the world, so they say. Fresh and new. I fell in love with Lain more every day, although I still didn't have the courage to say it. I think he understood that I loved him, and he politely respected my lack of words without any pressure or guilt.

We carried on, making the best of it and everything.

Aside from general housekeeping and lovemaking, the days consisted mostly of a lot of fiddling about trying to come up with new and exciting ways to entertain the pub patrons. It wasn't that the business was in dire need of a gimmick, but we thought it might be fun to spice things up a bit. A competitive event that wasn't pool playing and/or gossip. There's only so much gossip one can do to pass the time without becoming a general menace, and gimmicks were not something I thought about regularly, but Lain had some experience working in a variety of pubs and alehouses during his travelling days. He came up with the right brilliant idea that we should have a pub quiz night. The idea seemed appealing, so in a slapdash attempt to interject some levity, we decided to have one.

We really didn't have a clue what we were doing. The questions were ridiculous: How many head of sheep do the McInerny's graze in the east pasture on Tuesdays? What's the most popular cheese at O'dell's Old Cheese Shoppe? Even so, the evening was a smashing success. The place was packed, everyone brought their mates, and we gave away loads of free gargle and chips.

It was an exceedingly long and boisterous evening. No one wanted to leave, so we had to resort to a bit of pushing and shoving to get everyone off home. We locked down for the night round about half-one in the morning.

Apparently, pub-quiz is a rather shambolic affair. The place was in a sorry state, but cleaning up wasn't as tedious a task as it had first appeared. Lain is a wonderful dancer. He enjoys gloomy love songs too but favours his music a little less melancholy and a lot more vigorous. We thrashed about the place until we were so worn out that a cup of tea and a bath seemed like the idyllic end to the night, so we locked the doors and checked them twice, turned off the lights, and headed, stumbling over each other, up the stairs.

Once we'd reached the kitchen, Lain tripped over his laces as he attempted to cast off his shoes, then he tumbled into the wall, snapped on the kitchen light, and made straight for the tea and biscuits.

"Too many pints," he said.

"Not for me." All the whiskey and close dancing had me feeling a little bit randy. Tea was the last thing on my mind, and I was desperately trying to get his shirt off, pulling and tugging on the buttons, kissing him all the while as he fumbled to get the kettle on.

"Merle, for fuck sake, I am dying for cup of tea."

I just smiled at him and continued to kiss his neck until he gave his usual sigh of frustration.

"As you wish," I said as I did my out and out best to back away seductively. "But I'm going to go get out of these clothes. Don't be too long."

The provocative approach I had chosen didn't seem entirely convincing. I was giggling too damn much for the ploy to be effective, so I toddled off to the bathroom, still giggling as I turned on the shower and then stepped under the scrumptiously hot water…

Lain could take a beating.

He'd taken one almost every day as a child. Bullies. Old women with broomsticks who didn't like their veg stolen, but most had come at the hands of his various stepfathers. He had been violently set upon with pretty much anything one could imagine. Burned with cigarettes. Shot at. Pushed from a moving car, but never in his thirty-six years had he ever been stabbed…

As he entered the dark bedroom, it came out of nowhere.

A silent evil.

The blackest of eyes in the shadows.

He had often imagined how his end would come. A drifter's life isn't an easy life. The wrong place at the wrong time could happen at any time. Resignation is part of the deal. He had long ago reconciled the fear and uncertainty, but even acceptance doesn't prepare you for the inevitable. Never in a million moments in a million years had he ever actually thought, had any inkling or idea, that it would be like this.

Merle…

There had been plenty of women too, shop owners' daughters, farmers' wives and the like, beautiful, easy, eagerly looking for an exciting diversion, but none like Merle. She truly accepted him, no questions, no lectures, and no great expectations. How he loved her so.

"Merle," Lain whispered as he sank to the floor.

13

A Desperate Act *of Cleansing*

I stepped out of the shower then brushed the haze from the mirror over the sink. As I stood staring vacantly into my damp reflection, I wondered aloud where Lain could have gotten off to. I had hoped and expected that he would have joined me in the shower. The water was so silky-slick and warm, not to mention that I would have made it worth his while. No wait, I did mention it, passive aggressively and nonverbally, but I mentioned it all the same when I'd giggled my way out of the kitchen.

He was probably still out there, cigarette in hand, lights dimmed, mulling over his tea. I often found him like that, deep in contemplation over his teacup in the middle of the night. It worried me a bit, but I never had the nerve to ask what he was thinking about.

Was I afraid to know?

No, of course not, that was just rubbish paranoia, so I bounced out of the bathroom and down the hallway, but the breath of Lain's name never left off my lips. My throat felt crushed shut, and from behind, I caught a faint whisper in my ear: "It's time to settle up, Merle. How many men have to die for you, you ugly fuckin' mutt?" and as those words trailed off into the distance, the twinkling lights from a thousand derelict stars flooded my eyes.

When I came to, I could feel leather around my neck, a roar of blood in my ears. I was bent over the back of the sofa, hands bound, my face pressed into the cushions, and Mick was pacing back and forth. Pacing and mumbling. Mumbling incoherent drivel about what he perceived rightly belonged to him. He lurched in behind me, pressed his full weight against me. I could feel his filth running down my legs. He was so fuckin' disgusting. His touch no longer felt like the damnation I had so long hoped would be my salvation, and I thought about dying, about needing to. For the first time in my life, I *wanted* to die.

He took hold of the belt and began pulling and twisting, the entire time carrying on, spitting his tirade into the air, "Jon was fuckin' weak. He didn't appreciate what he had. He didn't fuckin' deserve it. Didn't deserve me as a friend. Didn't deserve you, you whore."

He always thought he could hurt me with those words, but he just sounded like a raving lunatic. A lunatic who was going to kill me. I had no breath left. Everything was becoming vague and shadowy, his words fading into the distance as he tried to throttle the life out of me. "He gave it to me, Merle. I didn't take anything. It was all supposed to be mine. He lost it fair and square, but NO, you couldn't be cooperative, could you, Merle? I tried to be nice in the beginning, but you, Merle, fuckin' bitch, sad sack Merle missed her dead fuckin' husband so much. Well, fuck you, Merle! And fuck your dead husband! See where it all gets you now!"

He pulled and pulled so hard on the leather that he lifted me up from the back of the sofa. Knees dangling above the floor, I felt weightless. I could see the entire universe in my mind, stars blinking, galaxies bursting with creation, everything swirling backwards, drawn into the black void in time…

I felt clean.

I felt worthy.

For the first time since Jon's death, I felt satisfied, and then the universe exploded.

All Mick heard in his last moment of breath was the click of the pistol and Lain's soft voice, "You will NEVER touch her again."

14

A Life *Changing*

I didn't really mind being in hospital over the holidays. I wasn't feeling particularly jubilant nor was I up to the task of feigning social graces either. For the most part, I was in and out of any sort of coherent state due to the drugs they were pumping into me. It was all very relaxing in the way the drugs made me care little about anything, though I did manage to overhear from the doctors and nurses that, in their professional opinion, Lain had suffered 'no serious lasting damage' to any of his internal organs from the stab wound, and he would ultimately recover. I did care about that, but not much else, including talking to the Garda. They had come by several times, snapping off words like 'self-defence' and 'no charges', and, as far as I could tell by putting together words that lingered long after they were gone, Mick was dead, dead as fuckin' dead can get. Apparently, Lain had splattered his head to bits all over my flat with Jon's pistol. Fair play to him. I only wished I could have seen that with my own eyes. Was it just a coincidence that Mick had taken the bullet I had always meant for myself? I started to wonder more about that and other things over the coming weeks.

I had shut myself up inside my own pain for so long that I'd stopped listening to the ether, stopped listening to my heart, my shadow, and even rational thought. The crushing guilt had become a prison cell, trapping me in the futility of a hollow disconnected life. I needed to find my centre of gravity again. I needed to get back to where I started. Strange that the journey would have led me here, to Lain's bedside. It continues to astonish me how strong he has become.

In the coming months of recuperation, Lain kept silent vigil over me, even during my most manic moments, one in which I dismantled the kissing room. It was time. Time to let Jon go, just like he'd wanted, and despite the delay, I finally relinquished his ashes to his parents. They chose to give him a proper burial in the family plot at the old cemetery. The service was lovely. We celebrated his life, and at that moment, I realised that the suffering had not been all mine to bear.

It took me the better part of several weeks to empty out the kissing room. I kept Jon's books, his eyeglasses, and one photograph of him with my father, which had been taken in the pub the month before we were married. Everything else, I insisted, needed to be burned and sent back to the fire that had given birth to his spirit.

Lain never spoke one single word, had not one complaint even through all of my hysterical, irrational, and altogether unnecessary explanations of why it had to be that way. It's amazing how we cling to life, to our memories, in desperation and in joyous nostalgia.

Speaking of history, I also have the most wonderful photo of Henry, Lain and I, taken during the pub quiz night, so long ago it seems now. Three people, unrelated, old and young, making a connection amongst the chaos of life: happy, contented, and blissfully unaware. Until now, I had been afraid to look at it, afraid of its alluring innocence and the dark it might reveal.

I didn't want to think about that night. Didn't want to stir up the dread or be haunted forever by the memories of that evening. In time though, I put my fears behind me and hung that photograph in the pub, right next to the one of me with my father and Jon. The dread had changed me somehow. They aren't just pictures to me anymore. They had become windows, and if you gaze *through* them, you can bear witness to the vast and unbounded power of the universe. If you stare at them long enough, you'll see love.

As the months drew on, a strange and wonderful calmness sank into our ordinary little lives. Gentle and comforting, it flowed through, around, and between everything. It filled in the ruptured spaces and gave us all a bit of peace in the dark.

15

Colour My World

There is just something miraculous about a
warm spring day. Its caress is the sweetly
scented breath of rebirth. A year and all its
chaos, horror, and joy had passed away on the wind,
taking with it all the moments of regret and despair.

I was in the grip of hysteric jubilance, so I had
decided, finally, to take Lain to see the cottage willed to
me by my father. On the outskirts of the village, it sits
nestled on a majestic cliff, backed by emerald green
rolling hills, with golden grasses swaying gracefully
along with the breeze, and sprawling tumbleweeds of
heather blooming in the mist. In my hopeful eyes, its
splendour as we pulled up was everything a storybook
would have described. Everything we had survived for.

Lain got out of the car and did a full circle turn with

his hands on his hips, nodding his head in approval. "I think this could really be something, Merle," he said, shielding his eyes from the rays of the sun as a million possibilities flooded his face.

I could feel his happiness hit me even from where I was stood. It felt wonderful.

Henry had thoroughly outdone himself in keeping the place up for me over the years. I don't know whether the friendship with my father or his paternal love for me compelled him to do it, but I was forever grateful. The small garden was tidy and noticeably looked after, and in spite of the linen dustsheets on all of the furniture, the interior of the cottage was neat as a new pin. Maybe it was my imagination, but it still smelled like pipe tobacco, leather, and old books, as if my father's spirit had never left the place. He was still there along with a tempest of memories stashed away in long forgotten hope chests packed with photographs, old clothes, children's toys, journals, and books. So many books. There was so much treasure to discover that Lain and I lost track of the day as we spent hours rummaging through the thousands of dust-laden trinkets. For me, this cottage was the embodiment of the spirit of my family, the very origins of my flesh and of my soul. For Lain, it was that of a life denied him. The promise of what could be was everywhere and in everything, right down to the dry and creaky floorboards. We both felt it, and so we let it sweep us away.

We fell about the place, stumbling over each other in our excitement. We took the curtains down, opened all the windows, dusted, and scrubbed clean every skirting board and insignificant crack and crevice until the place sparkled with our passion, and since it was such an exceptionally beautiful day, we took a short respite around noon and had lunch out on the cliffs in the warm embrace of the sun. After we ate, we ran through the sea-sprayed heather, cast pebbles kissed with wishes into the sea, then lazed about in the warm breeze. I remarked on how much I loved his smile, even with parsley in it, and he, with much earnestness, praised the egg sandwiches before our lips met and parted in a thousand different ways as we lay in the heather, paying no notice to the time, the drink, and who we once were.

The world simply got away from us, as it so often does for those in love, and considering that we were exhausted, filthy, and deranged with liquor and glee, we both agreed that we should stay for the night. The pub would be there in the morning, Henry would be only a wee bit irritated, maybe, probably, but no worse for the inconvenience, and we just didn't want to let the tranquillity of the moment slip away. As dusk drew in, we settled into its still serenity *and* the enormous antique four-poster mahogany bed that towers prominently in my father's bedroom. It's so prominent, so dominating in stature that it hardly allows for any other furniture in the room. With down blankets and pillows, it billowed around us, so soft and clean and clinging to the light, which was fading fast, but the little fireplace on the far wall cast such a warm romantic glow over the room when lit that I paid no mind to the darkness creeping in around us. I just closed my eyes, listened to the fire crackling, and let the soothing scent of home wash over me until I felt drowsy with contentment. Until I felt safe. My demon had finally been laid to rest, and I smiled at the thought. I was free, blissfully so, and I had almost let myself fold into it when Lain gently stroked the hair from my face.

"Merle," he whispered, his voice soft, his tone gentle

with affection. I opened my eyes and looked up into his. "So, Merle, do you think you might be, maybe a little bit in love with me yet?" he asked, but he sounded nervous, unsure he should have, so I reached up and caressed his face. I understood his fear. When everything has been taken from you, hope is a bitter torment, and it can stain a heart with delusion and desire. I didn't want to fall prey to delusion or desire either, so I too had refused to let myself hope. I knew all too well the tremor in his voice, and the choked-back tears in mine, but you have to take risks at some point.

"That might be, maybe, the most ridiculous question you've ever asked of me, you mad gorgeous fool. Thinking and knowing are two different things, Lain, and I know I'm in love with you. More than a little bit. There, I finally said it, and I mean it. I am deeply in love with you, and right now, it finally feels real enough to say. Real enough to feel. For the life of me, I still don't know why I've been so afraid of this, of you, of living."

I was feeling guilty for withholding the truth from him for so long, but he just started giggling as he withdrew from his query, and my answer. He might have even been blushing, but it was hard to tell with the fire and the blaze of sunset streaming through the window-panes. Everything was already flushed, and I guess in that moment, Lain had stopped being afraid too when he said, "Marry me, Merle."

In secret we'd met, and in the silence of spent lifeless hours we'd loved, and lost, and loved again, but in this moment, a moment finally without fear, we'd left precious little space for words, other than, "Yes."

About the Author

Cheryl Anne Gardner is a writer of dark, often disturbing art-house novellas and abstract flash fiction. Her love of literature began at an early age with Stoker's Dracula. Captivated by the Gothic and Dark Romantic stylings of Poe, Lovecraft, Kafka, and de Sade, her passion for the macabre manifests itself throughout her own work to this day. In 2010, she became enamoured with Flash Fiction and its experimental style, and she's been writing prolifically in the genre ever since. She enjoys exploring political, social, and psychological issues. Her flash fiction has been published in dozens of journals. When she isn't writing, she likes to chase marbles on a glass floor, eat lint, play with sharp objects, and make taxidermy dioramas with dead flies. She lives with her husband on the east coast USA, is an enthusiastic gardener, and dabbles in cement sculpture when she isn't spoiling her adopted feral cats.

You can find her work at various online retailers. Her novellas are available in print and in eBook formats.

Titles by Cheryl Anne Gardner

Knowing Joe
Kitsch
The Duskhouse
And Death Dreamt Us All
The Thin Wall
Logos
The Splendor of Antiquity

www.ingramcontent.com/pod-product-compliance
Lightning Source LLC
Chambersburg PA
CBHW020642130626
46552CB00003B/1364